Disney

CINDERELLA

Ladybird Books

Cinderella lived with her father, who loved her dearly. Her mother had died many years before, when Cinderella was just a baby.

After a time, Cinderella's father married again. His new wife was a widow who had two daughters of her own.

When Cinderella's father died, her stepmother and stepsisters made her their servant. They took away Cinderella's pretty clothes and made her do all the housework.

One day an invitation
arrived from the royal
palace. There was
going to be a ball,
and all the ladies in
the land were invited.

"We'll dance with the prince!" said the stepsisters excitedly.

"Yes," said their mother. "But Cinderella can't go to the ball, because *she* has nothing to wear."

But Cinderella's friends,
the birds and the mice,
found an old party dress
in the attic. It had
belonged to Cinderella's
mother. That night, as
Cinderella slept, they
gathered ribbons, sashes
and ruffles, and turned
the dress into a beautiful
ballgown.

On the evening of the ball Cinderella's stepsisters were furious when they saw how beautiful she looked. Shrieking with rage, they tore at her dress until it was in shreds.

Poor Cinderella stood weeping as the others left for the ball. She was crying so hard she didn't realise that someone was watching… her fairy godmother!

"Dry your eyes, my dear," said the fairy godmother. "You *shall* go to the ball!"

With a wave of her wand and a few magic words, Cinderella's fairy godmother turned a pumpkin into a splendid coach. The mice became horses and a driver.

Best of all, the fairy godmother turned Cinderella's tattered dress into a magnificent ballgown. She even put dainty glass slippers on Cinderella's feet.

"Have a wonderful time," said the fairy godmother. "But you must be home by midnight, for that's when the magic will end."

At the ball, the prince danced with Cinderella all evening. No one, not even her stepsisters, knew who Cinderella was.

Suddenly the clock began to strike twelve, and Cinderella remembered her fairy godmother's warning. She fled from the ballroom and ran down the palace steps. The prince ran after her, but all he found was one of her glass slippers.

By the time Cinderella reached the palace gates, her ballgown had changed back to rags, the coach was a pumpkin again, and the horses and driver were mice once more.

But Cinderella was still wearing one glass slipper.

The next day, the prince gave the glass slipper he had found to a messenger. "Find the girl whose foot fits this slipper," he said, "for she is my true love."

The messenger took the glass slipper to every house in the land. At last he came to Cinderella's house and Cinderella's stepsisters tried on the slipper. But no matter how hard they pushed and pulled it would not fit. Then, before Cinderella could try it on, the glass slipper fell to the floor and broke into a thousand pieces!

But Cinderella had the other glass slipper. She showed it to the messenger, and he saw how neatly it fitted her foot.

"This is wonderful!" he exclaimed. "You must come with me to the palace!"

The prince was overjoyed to
see his true love again, and he
asked Cinderella to marry him
at once. Filled with happiness,
she agreed. Everyone in the
kingdom was invited to the
wedding...

...and Cinderella and the prince
lived happily ever after.

Put the pictures in the right order to tell the story of Cinderella.

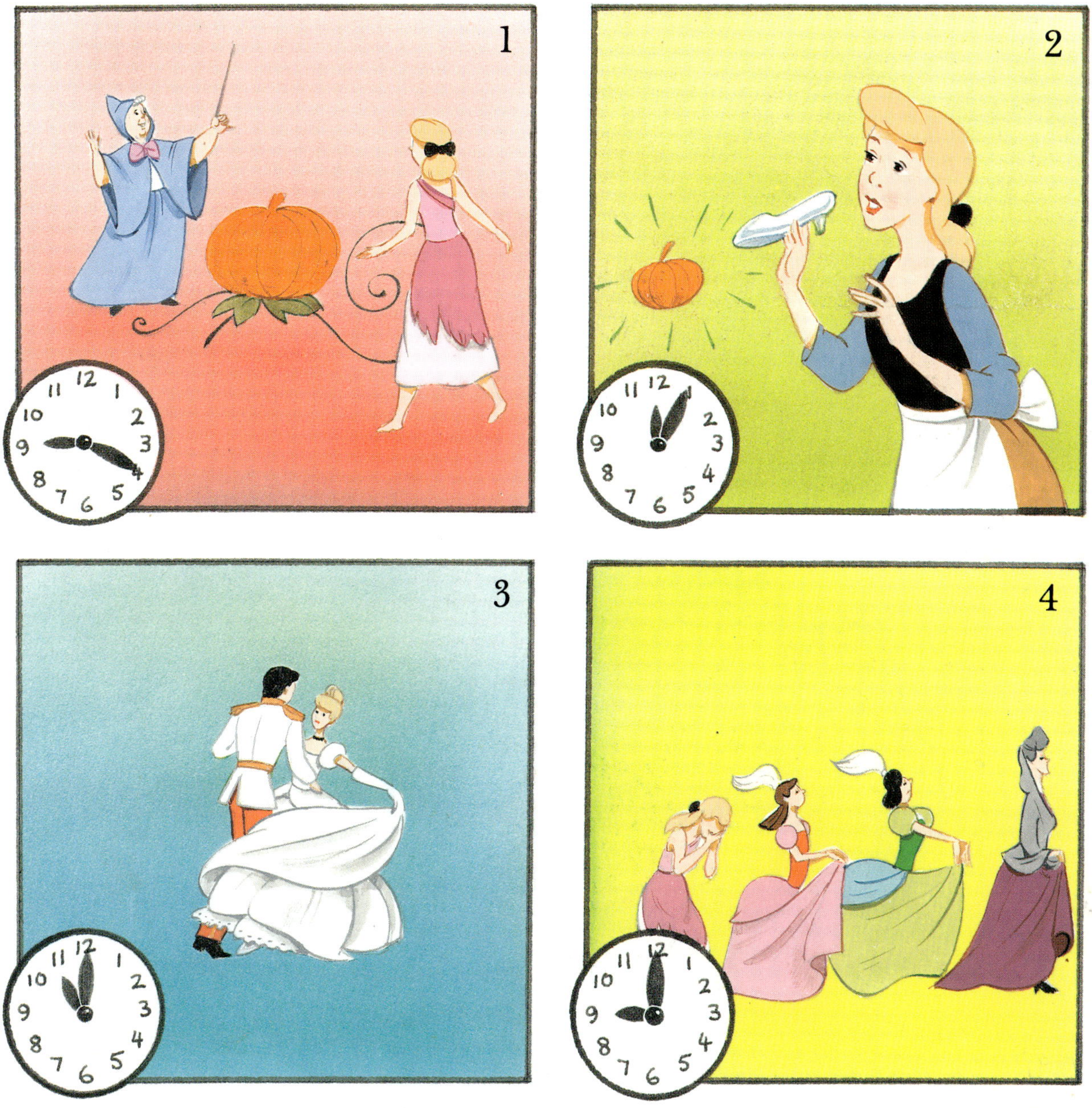

1

2

3

4

There are ten differences in the bottom picture. Can you find them?

Differences: Shape of hand mirror; necklace on stepsister; clock; tape measure; ball of wool; braid on cushion; Cinderella's bow; Cinderella's apron; wood panelling; feather on stepsister's head.

Which two Cinderellas are the same?

Which things will Cinderella take to the ball?

Match the shoe to the character.

1

2

3

Answers: Cinderella will take the ballgown and coach; stepsister — shoe 2; Cinderella — shoe 3; prince — shoe 1.

There are six mistakes in this picture. Can you find them?

Who do these shadows belong to?

A

B

C

D

E

F

Answer: A – mice; B – stepmother; C – prince; D – fairy godmother; E – Cinderella; F – stepsister.

Match the objects to the characters.

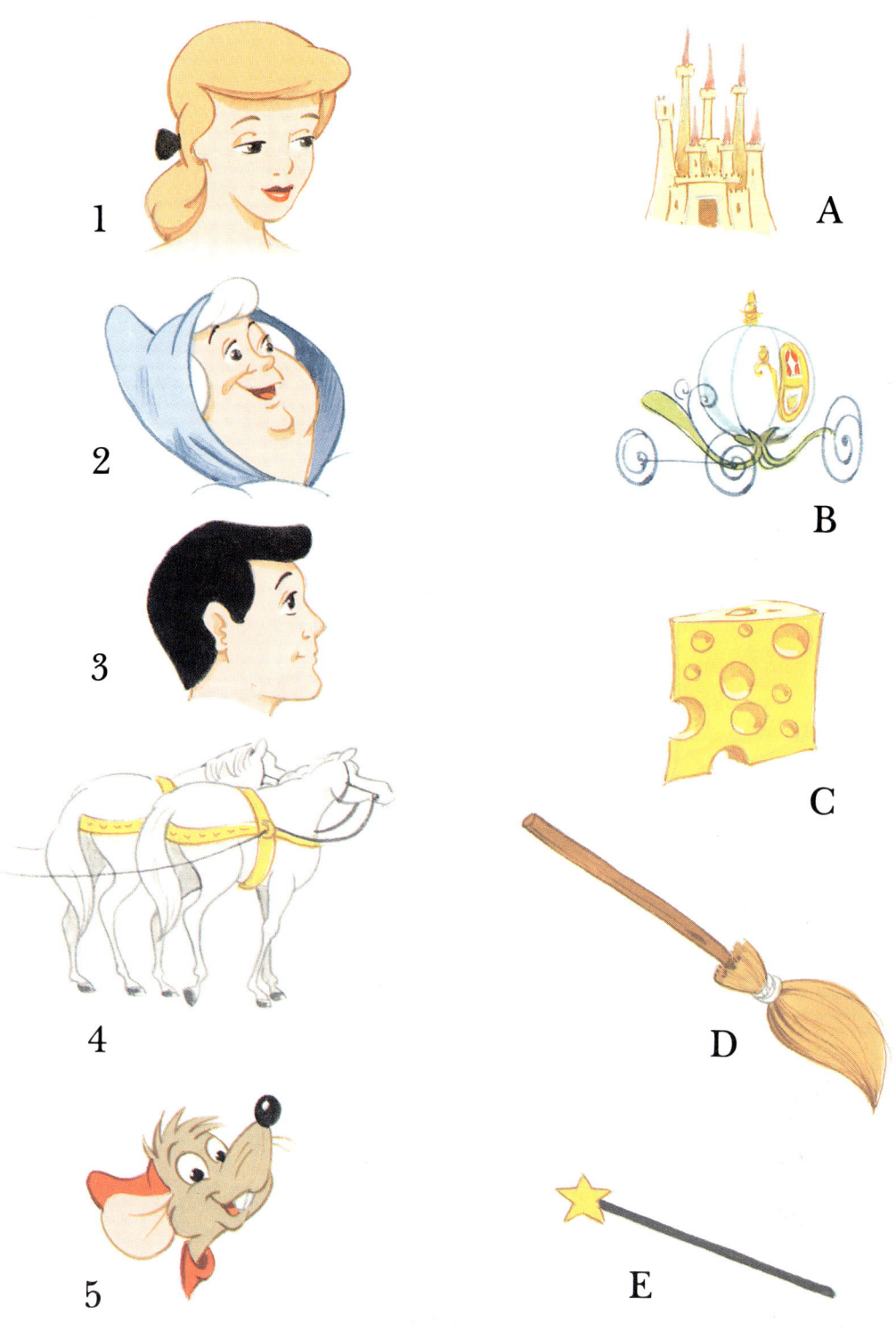

1

2

3

4

5

A

B

C

D

E

Can you find these objects in the picture?

1 pumpkin   2 ugly sisters   3 brooms

4 mice   5 cups   6 birds